Seldovia Sam

and the

Blueberry Bear

WRITTEN BY
Susan Woodward Springer

ILLUSTRATED BY
Amy Meissner

D1530528

Alaska Northwest Books®
Portland • Anchorage

To Caroline Emily Johnson. Read, Dream, Live!
— S. W. S.

For Brian, again.
— A. C. M.

Text © 2005 by Susan Woodward Springer
Illustrations © 2005 by Amy Meissner

Library of Congress Cataloging-in-Publication Data

Springer, Susan Woodward.
  Seldovia Sam and the blueberry bear / written by Susan Woodward Springer ; illustrated by Amy Meissner.
      p. cm. – (The misadventures of Seldovia Sam ; 4)
  Summary: Sam dreads the first day of school and his annual back-to-school essay, but an encounter with a bear cub while picking blueberries gives him an exciting topic.
  ISBN 0-88240-603-5 (softbound)
  [1. First day of school—Fiction. 2. Schools—Fiction. 3. Bears—Fiction. 4. Blueberries—Fiction.] I. Meissner, Amy, ill. II. Title III. Series: Springer, Susan Woodward. Misadventures of Seldovia Sam ; 4.
  PZ7.S768465Scm 2005
  [Fic]—dc22   2005018436

Alaska Northwest Books®
An imprint of Graphic Arts Center Publishing Company
P.O. Box 10306, Portland, Oregon 97296-0306
503-226-2402 • www.gacpc.com

President: Charles M. Hopkins
General Manager: Douglas A. Pfeiffer
Associate Publisher: Sara Juday
Editorial Staff: Timothy W. Frew, Tricia Brown, Kathy Howard,
    Jean Bond-Slaughter
Production Staff: Richard L. Owsiany, Susan Dupere

Editor: Michelle McCann
Cover design: Andrea L. Boven / Boven Design Studio, Inc.; Elizabeth Watson
Interior design: Andrea L. Boven / Boven Design Studio, Inc.; Jean Andrews

Contents

Arctic Circle

Yukon River

Susitna River

**Bering
Sea**

Kuskokwim River

Mount △
McKinley

Anchorage

Homer

SELDOVIA

Kodiak

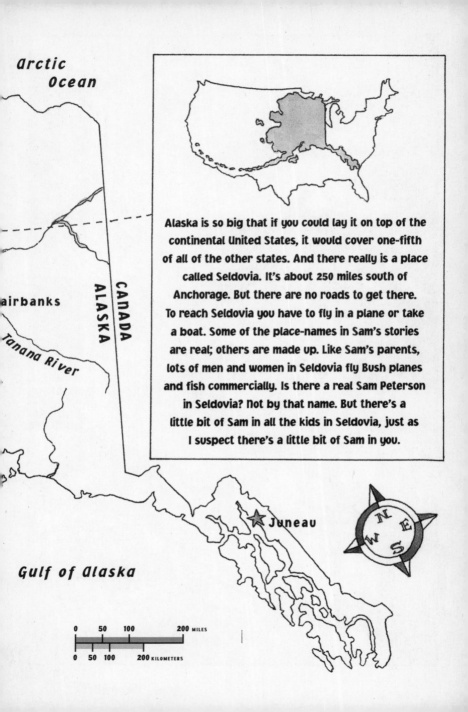

Arctic Ocean

Fairbanks

Tanana River

CANADA

ALASKA

Alaska is so big that if you could lay it on top of the continental United States, it would cover one-fifth of all of the other states. And there really is a place called Seldovia. It's about 250 miles south of Anchorage. But there are no roads to get there. To reach Seldovia you have to fly in a plane or take a boat. Some of the place-names in Sam's stories are real; others are made up. Like Sam's parents, lots of men and women in Seldovia fly Bush planes and fish commercially. Is there a real Sam Peterson in Seldovia? Not by that name. But there's a little bit of Sam in all the kids in Seldovia, just as I suspect there's a little bit of Sam in you.

Juneau

N E W S

Gulf of Alaska

| 0 | 50 | 100 | | 200 MILES |

| 0 | 50 | 100 | 200 KILOMETERS |

1

The Blueberry Blues

August in Seldovia was both the best month and the worst month. It was the best because salmonberries, blueberries, and high bush cranberries were ripe. It was the worst because school started at the end of it.

Sam looked around the dusty shed and sighed a big sigh. It was so big it startled Trouble Cat from her nap atop a pile of fishing nets. The cat hopped onto Sam's shoulder and hitched a ride out of the shed, as Sam juggled blueberry buckets and bright orange hand rakes. Neptune spotted the berry picking gear and danced with excitement. Sam had never seen a dog so crazy about eating blueberries!

Sam was not looking forward to school. He knew the first assignment would be to write an essay on something he did over the summer. Judges would read the essays and give cash prizes to the winners. Sam sighed again. He sure could use some money to buy the X-Treme Trail Smasher bike he wanted so badly. Last year he almost saved enough, but then he lost Billy Sutton's bike in the wildfire and gave him his savings to buy a new one.

But there was no chance Sam could win. He hadn't done anything exciting this summer. He'd fished on the *Wild Rose* with Dad. He camped in his driftwood fort at Sandy Cove. He'd flown with Mom in her Cessna delivering freight. All of that had been fun but none of it was exciting enough to win the essay contest.

Sam's know-it-all classmate, Melody Chambers, had already informed him that she had been to ballet camp *(lah-di-dah,* thought Sam) with famous dancers from New York City *(lah-di-double-dah,* thought Sam). Sam was afraid she would read her essay, throw in a few French words and win the contest hands down.

Neptune nudged Sam's leg, reminding him it was time to go. Mom was driving Sam and Billy out the old logging road to pick blueberries. It had been a day-before-school tradition in their family for as long as Sam could remember.

Just then Billy flew into the yard on his bike, skidding to a stop and crashing into Mom's flowerpots. "Hi Sam," said Billy with a big grin. He hopped off his bike and set the pots upright. "Sorry I'm late. You got the buckets and stuff?"

"In here," said Sam, patting his backpack.

"Let's go! I can taste those blueberries now!"

They rode through town and down the hill to the airstrip to wait for Mom to land. As they coasted to the hangar, Sam spotted her plane coming in. Then he noticed her Jeep parked nearby.

Oh no! One of the rear tires was as flat as a sand dollar!

"Billy, look!" cried Sam, pointing at the tire.

"No problem, Sam. We'll just get the spare out of the back and help your Mom change it. We'll be picking berries before you know it."

"'Fraid not. Mom's spare tire is in Homer getting fixed. We're not going anywhere."

Billy's shoulders slumped. He was always cheerful and it was almost impossible to make him sad.

Except for maybe now . . .

2

The Terrible Truck

Mom taxied her plane up to the hangar and cut the engine. She jumped out, clutching a paper sack. "Hi boys. I brought donut holes. You hungry?" she asked.

Billy's eyes lit up. He was always hungry.

Mom turned to Sam. "Did you bring the blueberry rakes, Sam?"

"Yep. But Mom . . ." Sam began.

"What?" she asked.

"Your tire is flat," he said in a small voice.

Mom looked at the rear tire. "Oh dear."

"Hey, Mrs. Peterson," Billy broke in, "Let's just borrow Mr. Peterson's truck."

"Good idea, but we can't. Sam's father drove his truck to Jakolof Bay this morning to cut firewood." Mom shook her head. "I guess we'll just have to wait until this weekend to go berry picking."

Sam and Billy looked at each other in alarm. Miss their special day-before-school-starts berry picking?! No way!!

Both talking at once, Sam and Billy begged Mom to borrow a car to take them berry picking. The boys pushed their bikes as Mom walked beside them back into town. When they passed the Tidepool Café, Sam spotted Charlie Dreyer's rattletrap old pickup truck.

"Mom!" cried Sam, "Charlie will let us borrow his truck. I know he will!" Charlie was Mom's boss at the flying service in Homer.

"Sam, that's an awful truck," protested Mom. It was true. The once-red paint had long ago faded to a dirty pink spotted with rust. The tailpipe was attached with wire that trailed on the ground. The windshield was cracked and one of the headlights was smashed. And inside, the cab needed some serious housekeeping.

Sam and Billy dropped their bikes and burst into the Tidepool. Sam spotted Charlie at his regular table along with Danny, who ran the road grader and the snowplow.

"Hi-Charlie-Mom's-car-has-a-flat-can-we-borrow-your-truck-to-go-berry-picking-please?" Sam's words came out all in a rush.

"Hi Sam. Nice to see you too," Charlie said with a slow grin. Sam was dying to get going, but there was no rushing Charlie. "Got a flat, Rose?" he continued.

"Yes," said Mom, "and the spare's being fixed. Walt's got the truck out at Jakolof, probably half full of firewood by now."

"Firewood," said Danny, "That's what I oughta be doing today ..."

Sam shifted on his feet. They could be

here all day! "So Charlie, do you think we could borrow your truck, just for a couple of hours? This is the last day we have to pick berries before school starts."

"Sure, Sam," Charlie said slowly, "But what about bears? Danny just told us about giving some tourists a ride into town yesterday. They were out hiking and a bear chased them. Scared them half to death."

Mom turned to Danny. "Half to death," he nodded. "It was a big one."

Charlie added, "Bear stood on his hind legs and pawed the air." He stood up and waved his coffee cup and growled.

Sam could see she was about ready to cancel their trip. "But Mom, we have Neptune. She'll keep bears away," he pleaded. Mom's face softened but she still didn't look convinced.

"Not true, Sam," said Charlie. "Dogs can stir up a bear who's minding his own business."

"Okay, okay, we'll leave Neptune in the truck! Pleasemom, pleasemom, pleasemom," Sam chanted in desperation. Billy joined in, and the men at the table started laughing.

It worked! Mom gave in! "Alright boys, we'll go but you'll have to stick close to me. No wandering off!"

"No problem, Mom. Thanks Charlie!" Sam called as he and Billy ran outside.

They opened the door of the cab and tossed in their backpacks and the bag of donut holes. They piled in with Neptune, then Mom climbed in and turned the key in the ignition. A rich gasoline smell made her wrinkle her nose. "Phew, Charlie ought to have this thing tuned!" she muttered.

She drove the truck to the dirt road that ran to the head of Seldovia Bay and the blueberry fields. As they drove, the dust from the road boiled up and poured into the cab through little rust holes in the floor.

Mom choked and sputtered, "Ugh. I can barely see. Borrowing this truck was a mistake."

"Here Mom," offered Sam, "I'll roll down a window." Together, he and Billy wrestled with the stubborn old hand crank and managed to roll the passenger window down. But instead of helping, it just made things worse. Dust poured in and filled the cab.

"Now I can't see a thing!" cried Mom, pulling over. "I'm turning around and going home!" In all that dust, Sam couldn't see her face, but he could tell by her voice that she was out of patience.

Had they gone to all this trouble just to turn around and go home again? Sam wanted to beg and plead one more time but he knew that was a bad idea with Mom so cross. He and Billy were very quiet as they wondered what would happen next.

3

Berries, Berries
Everywhere

After a few moments, the air inside the cab cleared and they could see out the window. The landscape was beautiful—rolling hills thick with bushes and here and there a young spruce tree. Sam realized they were on the edge of the blueberry fields! They had made it after all!

Sam looked over at Mom, and her face broke into a big smile. "Well boys, looks like you got your wish." She got out of the truck and shut her door.

Billy let out a whoop, and he and Sam scrambled over each other to retrieve their backpacks from behind the seat. In their hurry, they knocked the bag of donut holes to the floor. Neptune dove into this unexpected treat, and the boys tumbled out of the truck and slammed the door.

They ran to where Mom stood in a swampy meadow surrounded by hills. Blueberries hung like big blue gumballs from tall bushes in the meadow. On the hillsides, the berry bushes were even bigger but the hills were thick with alder and elderberry bushes, and small spruce trees as well.

"Sam, you and Billy stay down in the meadow where I can keep an eye on you. Don't climb the hills. The brush is too dense and a bear wouldn't see you until it was almost on top of you."

"Sure, Mom," agreed Sam as he and Billy pulled out their berry rakes and buckets. Instead of handles, the buckets had long strings so you could hang them around your neck and leave both hands free to pick berries.

"Bet I can fill my bucket first," challenged Billy.

"You're on," said Sam, and they each ran to a berry-laden bush and began scooping the fat blueberries off the branches.

The late summer sun warmed the meadow, and magpies and crows flew about. The boys settled into a quiet rhythm of picking, moving from bush to bush across the meadow. Sam stopped a moment to stretch his arms. He looked up and spotted a huge bush full of berries just up the hill from where he stood. He forgot Mom's instructions and climbed up to the big bush. He noticed that beyond it were more big bushes full of berries. And beyond that, even more . . . He picked a little and climbed a little and picked a little and climbed a little.

Sam didn't realize how far he'd gone from the meadow until he stood up and looked for Mom and Billy. He could just make out their heads . . . way down below him! Uh oh! Better get back down the hill!

Just then, the bushes next to Sam rustled and sticks cracked. "Neptune?" he whispered. No dog appeared, but the rustling stopped. Come to think of it, he hadn't seen Neptune for quite a while. The bushes rustled again. Was it a squirrel? Sam could feel his heart beating.

Suddenly, a large black and white magpie burst from the bushes, flew up, and perched on a branch above Sam. It cocked its head and chattered at him. *Phew,* thought Sam, *false alarm.*

Then another stick cracked and the magpie took off.

Sam froze.

Who's in the Bushes?

The bushes rustled again. "Hello?" asked Sam in a wavery voice. No answer. The wind blew and the bushes rustled again.

Sam chuckled with relief. *It was the wind rustling the bushes,* he thought, *that's all.* Sam picked some more. There were so many berries here he just couldn't leave yet. Just one more branch and he'd head back downhill.

Sam picked and picked. His bucket was almost full. He was sure to beat Billy now. The bushes moved and Sam heard . . . chewing??! "Neptune!" he called softly.

Neptune liked to pull berries from the lowest branches with her teeth and eat them.

More rustling. "Billy?" tried Sam. "Quit fooling around. You're scaring me!" Sam looked around nervously. No, he could still see Billy's red baseball cap at the bottom of the hill.

"Hello?" Sam croaked. The chewing sound was getting louder and louder and . . .

Sam peered around a small spruce tree and came face-to-face with a bear cub! They stared at each other for a moment, then the cub moved closer. Even though it was still a baby it was as big as Sam.

Sam waved his blueberry rake at the cub. "Stop right there," he warned. But the curious cub smelled Sam's bucket of juicy berries. It kept coming toward him. Sam took a big step backward, then turned to make his escape. There, just twenty feet behind him was the mother bear! She stood on her hind legs. All Sam could see was a mountain of black fur.

Instantly, Sam forgot everything he'd ever learned about what to do in a bear encounter. He forgot to be quiet. He forgot to be calm. He forgot to move away slowly. Sam yelped and threw his blue-berry rake in the air. He spun around, and the bucket hanging from his neck swung out and caught on a tree branch. When Sam tried to run, he was caught by the bucket! In a panic, he yanked himself away from the tree. The string broke and the bucket fell to the ground, but Sam was free!

"Help, help!" yelled Sam as he barreled down the hill. The flying blueberry rake spooked the bear cub and it took off too, running down the hill alongside Sam! The mother bear wanted to stay near her cub so she chased Sam and the little bear down the hill as well.

Sam's legs were moving so fast he couldn't even feel his feet touch the ground. He could hear Neptune barking off in the distance. *Where is she when I need her?* Sam wondered.

Run Run Run!!

What the . . . ?!" yelled Billy as Sam and the two bears raced by him.

"Holy smokes!" screamed Mom as they approached.

Just then Sam tripped over a stump and fell headlong into some bushes. *That's it,* he thought, *I'm a goner.* He braced himself for a bear bite on the rear end . . . or worse!

Something jumped onto the middle of his back. "Aaahhhhiiieeee," screeched Sam, and he rolled, expecting to see black fur and giant teeth. But it was Neptune! Sam sat up quickly. The bears had run right on past him and were headed up the hill on the other side of the meadow, pursued by Neptune.

What took her so long!?! Sam thought with relief.

Billy and Mom ran to Sam. Mom was very upset. Billy looked upset too. "Geez, Sam, I thought you were a goner," he said, his eyes big and his face serious.

Mom grabbed Sam and hugged him—hard. Then came the lecture. "Sam, what were you thinking?" cried Mom. "No wait— you *weren't*

thinking and you weren't listening either. What did I say about climbing the hill? What have we always taught you about encountering a bear? That's it. We're going home right now. I'm not staying out here with a boy who's not grown up enough to obey directions!"

Sam winced. "And where's your berry rake? Where's your bucket?" she asked.

Sheepishly, Sam pointed up the hill. "Uh, I guess I dropped them," he offered.

"Well, I guess they'll have to stay there. You boys head back to the truck. I need to find Neptune. She's probably chased those bears a mile away by now."

"Mom, *please please* let me go get my bucket. It's full of berries and I know right where it is. Besides, it's kind of on the way to the truck," Sam pleaded.

Mom looked hard at Sam. She turned and looked hard at the hill where

Neptune had chased the bears. It was in the opposite direction from where the boys wanted to go, and there was no sign of bears. "Okay, Sam," she said, "But go quickly and then head right for the truck and stay there."

"Will do!" replied Sam.

"Do you really think they're gone?" Billy asked Sam quietly, when they were out of Mom's hearing. "I sure hope so," said Sam. "That was pretty scary. The cub was cute, but then when I turned around and saw the mother right behind me . . . I thought I was gonna be a bear snack."

"When I saw you flying down into the meadow with two bears chasing you, I thought we were all done for," agreed Billy as they trudged up the hill.

"All I can say is thank goodness for Neptune," said Sam. "I wonder how she got out of the truck . . ."

Billy broke in, "Boy, these berries are huge!"

"I know," replied Sam, "I saw them and that's why I came up here." He remembered his bet with Billy and realized any hope of winning was probably shot. His berries must have scattered everywhere when his bucket fell.

They reached the clump of bushes where Sam had been picking and found his bright orange berry rake easily, since it stood out against the green leaves. Not far away, Sam spotted his bucket lying on the ground. Amazing! Most of the berries were still inside!

Billy helped Sam scoop up the berries that had rolled out. "Your mom sure is mad," he said. "Yeah," agreed Sam, "She . . ."

Sam was interrupted by the sound of commotion down in the meadow. Mom was waving her arms and shouting.

Now what?

6

More Trouble

Mom looked up the hill and saw the boys. "Stay where you are," she called. "The bear cub came back. It was trying to get into Billy's berry bucket."

The boys stopped in their tracks. "Oh no," groaned Billy, "My berries!"

But Sam pointed out that his mom was carrying two buckets. "Looks like your berries are safe and sound."

"Sam, Billy—don't come down into the meadow," Mom instructed. "That bear cub is still around here someplace." She pointed with her arm. "Just head straight for the truck from where you are."

Sam and Billy turned and started toward the road and the truck in the direction Mom had pointed. She called out again, "Don't stop to fool around, you two. As soon as I find Neptune I'll meet you at the truck."

"Okay, Mom," called Sam. He and Billy reached the crest of the hill. They looked around at the landscape spread out below them. There, barely visible through some high alder bushes, was the dirt road, and they could just make out the faded pink of the hood of the truck. Hurray!

"I wonder where those blueberry bears are hiding?" teased Sam. He poked Billy in the back and grunted like a bear.

"Aah!" cried Billy, before he realized it was Sam making the bear noise. "Stop it. That's not funny." Sam crossed his eyes, stuck out his lower teeth, and made a bear-monster face. Billy started to giggle,

nervously, then he poked Sam back and grunted his own bear grunt.

The boys descended the hill through the thick brush, grunting and poking each other and laughing. At the bottom, the bushes grew so tall and so close together they couldn't see a thing.

"I think the road is this way," said Sam.

"I think it's over that way," pointed Billy.

"We should have figured this out when we were on top of the . . ." began Sam, but he was interrupted by a sudden crashing in the bushes very close to them.

They couldn't see a thing. Crash, crash! It was coming right at them.

"Ohmegod, ohmegod!" yelled Billy. "Bears!"

He grabbed Sam. The thick brush exploded next to them and something black shot out.

"Bears—aahhh!" cried Sam.

But it was Neptune! Neptune, what a relief!

Sam and Billy grabbed each other and collapsed, screaming with laughter. Neptune barked and licked their faces.

Mom heard the crashing and screaming and barking. "Sam! Billy!" she hollered. "Are you okay? Somebody answer me NOW!"

Neptune's ears perked up when she heard Mom. She turned and bounded through the bushes. Still gasping with laughter and trying to answer, the boys followed her.

"We're fine, Mom," Sam called as he pushed aside some branches. There was the road and there was the truck, and there was Mom. She looked about as upset and mad as Sam had ever seen her. Sam's smile disappeared.

"In the truck, boys. I've had enough of your silliness for one day."

For once Sam didn't protest or try to explain his way out of a situation. Quietly the boys loaded their gear into the truck and climbed in, as Neptune jumped in the back.

Mom got behind the wheel and turned the key. Nothing happened. The engine didn't growl and roar to life. No gasoline smell filled the cab. Nothing. Just a little "click-click-click" sound when she turned the key in the ignition.

Mom tried again. And again. Nothing but "click-click-click." "I cannot believe this," she muttered.

Sam and Billy were silent. This was turning out to be more adventure than they'd bargained for. What else could go wrong?

7

Stuck in the Truck

Billy, Mom, and Sam sat in the cab of Charlie's broken-down old truck. Just as Sam was thinking nothing else could happen to make things worse, the mother bear and her cub burst out of the bushes and loped across the dirt road ahead of them. They disappeared into the brush on the other side of the road. Neptune whined. Billy let out a startled, "Aah!"

When will those bears leave us alone? thought Sam.

"You two stay put," said Mom, opening her door. "I'm going to look under the hood and see if I can figure out what's wrong." Mom wasn't a mechanic, but from years of working on her Bush plane she knew something about engines.

"Your mom's awesome," admired Billy. Billy's mom didn't even like to put gas in their car, much less look under the hood.

Mom raised the hood and poked around. After a few minutes she stuck her head in the window of the cab. "The engine won't start because the distributor cap popped off. Would you boys look in there and see if you can find something I can use to wire it back in place?"

"Sure," said Sam, and he and Billy combed through all the junk on Charlie's dashboard and the floor of the cab. There were airplane parts, leftover take-out meals, unpaid bills, notes and pencil stubs, several very dirty coffee cups, and a set of greasy coveralls. And that was just the top layer!

Sam had an idea. "Wasn't there some wire hanging off the tailpipe?" he asked. "Yeah, I think so," replied Billy. He and Sam opened the door and slid out quietly. They went around to the back of the truck and looked underneath. Sure enough, there was a length of wire that seemed like it was extra.

Sam and Billy bent the wire back and forth to break it but it wouldn't break. "Give it a yank," suggested Billy, and so Sam did. Off came the wire, but the tailpipe thudded to the ground with it!

Mom's head shot up from underneath the hood. "What's that noise? What are you boys doing outside the truck?"

Sheepishly, Sam held up the wire with the broken tailpipe attached. "Um, we found some wire for you, Mom." He grinned.

Mom looked at the rusty tailpipe with the wire wound around it. Slowly her frown turned into a grin and her grin turned

into a laugh. "This is just too much!" Sam and
Billy laughed with her, and Sam brought
her the tailpipe and wire.

Mom pulled and this time the wire was
weakened enough so it broke off easily.

She wrapped wire around the distributor cap and tried to cinch it tight. Snap! The distributor cap broke clean in two pieces. Now they really weren't going anywhere!

"We could walk home," suggested Billy, trying to be helpful.

"No way," Mom shot back. "It's almost four miles to town, and there's no telling where those bears have gone to."

She has a point, thought Sam. *But how will we get home?*

8

Road Grader Rescue

Mom left the hood of the truck open and they all climbed into the cab. They sat quietly, trying to figure out what to do. They were so quiet Sam could hear Billy's stomach growling. So could Mom.

"Where's that sack of donut holes?" she asked.

"I think Neptune got them," said Sam. They looked in the back. Neptune was fast asleep in the sun, full of donut holes and bear-chasing adventure.

"Is that an engine I hear?" wondered Billy.

"No, it's just your stomach growling!" teased Sam. He and Billy poked and pushed each other.

"Wait a minute, boys—stop. I think Billy's right," said Mom.

They listened. Sure enough, it was an airplane engine, and it was coming closer. Charlie's yellow plane came into view overhead. From somewhere in the mess on the floor of the cab a radio crackled. Sam could hear Charlie's muffled voice.

"Find that radio!" cried Mom, and the boys pawed through the debris.

"Got it!" called Billy, pulling a portable radio out of the pocket of Charlie's work coveralls. He handed it to Mom.

"Charlie, Charlie, this is Rose. Do you read me?" she spoke into the radio.

"I copy you, Rose. I'm en route to Windy Bay. Good thing I spotted you—looks like you've had a breakdown." Charlie had seen the truck with the raised hood from the air and knew something was wrong. "You waiting for bears to come fix the truck?"

"Charlie, this truck is a nightmare!" scolded Mom. "The distributor cap came off and broke in two, and now the tailpipe is off also."

The radio chuckled. "Guess it might be time for a new truck," said Charlie. "I think Danny is driving the road grader somewhere around here. I'll try to raise him on the radio and get him to pick you up."

"Thanks Char ...," began Mom, but she was interrupted by another voice on the radio.

"Hey Charlie, I copied your radio call," he said. "I was headed to town but as soon as I turn this thing around I'll go out and pick them up."

"Roger that. Thanks, Danny. November 1-7-1 Delta clear," crackled Charlie as he signed off.

"Thanks, Danny. I'm clear," echoed Mom as she signed off too.

It was just a few minutes before Danny and the road grader roared up the road toward them. Danny ground to a halt and opened the door of the cab high above them.

They climbed up the ladder into the cab. The cab was small—maybe the size of a telephone booth—and Mom and Sam and Billy were wedged in tightly behind Danny. Neptune managed to scramble up and squeeze in by Mom's feet.

Danny grinned. "I don't normally pick up hitchhikers, but I hear there are some hungry bears in the area," he said with a wink. "Very funny," said Mom, trying not to smile.

Twenty minutes later they were back in Seldovia, dusty and rattled but safe. They thanked Danny for the ride, walked Billy

to the clinic where his mom worked, and then headed home.

Sam was exhausted. Dad had cooked steaks on the grill—Sam's favorite dinner. Normally he would have devoured his steak and talked nonstop to Dad all about his adventures. But tonight, Sam was almost too tired to eat.

When he finally dropped into bed, Sam sighed. The soft blanket, the cool pillow—he could feel himself drifting . . . off. . . . If only . . . the first . . . day . . . of school . . . wasn't tomorrow . . . and oh-my-gosh-the-essay-contest! Sam's eyes flew open and he began to worry. Then, he realized the day had given him a great topic. He smiled sleepily, closed his eyes again, and fell . . . into . . . a deep . . . blueberry . . . sleep . . .

9

Essay Day

In the morning, Sam awoke with a feeling of dread. Summer was over! No more freedom, no more fun! Aaagh! Even the bowl of blueberries with cream he had for breakfast wasn't enough to make up for his first-day-of-school blues!

Sam trudged to school. On the playground, Sam could see Melody acting like a princess, turning pirouettes and showing off her ballet moves. Then Sam spotted Billy. "Hey," said Sam.

"Hey yourself," replied Billy. "How are you feeling after our big adventure yesterday?"

49

"Tired," Sam answered. "And worried about the essay contest. What're you going to write about?"

"Can't tell you." Billy said with a grin, "It's a surprise." Sam got a funny feeling in his stomach. What if Billy wrote about the blueberry bears too? Billy was a much better writer than Sam. If Billy chose the same topic, Sam didn't have a prayer of winning that cash prize!

"How about you?" asked Billy.

"Umm, I don't know," Sam mumbled.

Sam was relieved to hear the bell ring. He and Billy and all the other students raced to their classrooms. Everyone had until the end of the day to write their essay: "What I Did This Summer." At the end of the day, they would hand in their essays to the teacher.

Then a group of community leaders gathered to read the essays and pick the eight best writers. Those eight students got to read their essays at a special assembly on Saturday night. It was a big deal and most of the town filled the bleachers in the school gym to listen and find out who would win the grand prize.

All day, Sam wrote and wrote. He did a lot of erasing too. He broke his pencil twice and had to resharpen it. He told the story of the blueberry bears like he was writing a letter to his grandmother. He tried to remember all the details and make his story as exciting as the day had been. Sam handed in his finished essay just as the 3 o'clock bell rang.

Billy caught up with Sam outside. "Hey Sam, want to go fish for salmon off the bridge? Darwin has some new lures we can use." Darwin Chambers, Melody's cousin, was as nice as Melody was bossy.

"Sounds good," agreed Sam, but he was

still worried. "Hey Billy, what *did* you write about anyway?" he added.

"I told you already, Sam. It's a big hairy surprise!" Billy shouted as he took off on his bike. "C'mon! We've got fish to catch!"

Sam peddled after Billy. *A HAIRY surprise?* he wondered. *Billy must have written about the bears, for sure!*

Sam was unusually quiet for the rest of the afternoon. They fished and each of the boys caught a salmon. Sam rode his bike home with one hand, holding the big fish by its gills in the other. With no gears and just one hand, it was hard to ride up the last little hill to his house. He wished more than anything he could win the contest prize money and buy a new bike. But how could he win if Billy wrote about the bears too?

During the next few days, Sam saw some of the essay contest judges around Seldovia: Mrs. Dodge, the white-haired librarian, the town doctor, Dr. Stott, Mr. Farnham, the mayor, and Mr. Fenwick, a retired school-teacher. They all smiled at Sam. Did their smiles mean something? Or were they just being friendly? By Friday, Sam was glad the week was over.

That night before bed, Sam pulled out his old stuffed black bear from the back of his closet. He was too old for sleeping with toys, but something made him want to prop the saggy old bear on his pillow.

"Wish me luck!" he whispered.

10

The Contest Surprise

On Saturday morning, Sam raced his bike to the Post Office. That's where the winners were posted. If it was going to be bad news, Sam wanted to be sure he saw it before anyone else.

But it was too late. As Sam pedaled into the parking lot, Danny drove by in the road grader and called out, "Congratulations, Sam."

Congratulations? thought Sam as he jumped off his bike.

There was the notice. And there was his name! "Sam Peterson—Encounter with Blueberry Bears." He scanned the list. There was Melody Chambers, no surprise. Mary Rutledge, Ian Hatcher, a few more names, and . . . "Billy Sutton—Ancient Treasures at Fossil Point."

Fossil Point! Ancient Treasures! No bears? Hey, maybe he had a chance to win after all! Or did he? Fossils and ancient treasures sounded pretty interesting.

By the time Sam got home again, Mom and Dad already knew he was a finalist. News traveled quickly in Seldovia.

"Good job, Sam," Dad said. "We can't wait to hear your essay tonight."

Then it hit Sam—he'd have to get up in front of the whole town and read. Yikes!

By dinnertime, Sam was so nervous he could hardly eat. He pushed food around his plate, and then put on the clean shirt Mom handed him. They arrived at the school gym for the assembly to find it was already crowded.

Sam's teacher steered him up on stage to sit with the other finalists. Sam slid into a seat next to Billy. To his dismay, Melody sat down on his other side. She was wearing a ballet tutu and some funny shoes!

"I'm going to read in costume," Melody announced. "It will help bring my words to life!"

Sam rolled his eyes. "How about you, Sam," Melody teased, "Where's your bear costume?" Sam scowled but was saved from having to respond when the school principal announced the start of the program.

Mary Rutledge was first, reading about helping her dad hang wallpaper. It was a very funny essay—Mary wrote about how she stepped in the bucket of wallpaper paste and went flying over backwards, bringing the wet wallpaper down on top of her. The audience laughed a lot.

Melody was next. Her essay was full of big French words, which she pronounced flawlessly. She demonstrated some of the ballet moves, even standing on the tips of those funny shoes. Secretly Sam was impressed. So was the audience, which clapped loudly.

Three more readers, and then Sam. He stood up and began to read. After a couple of sentences, he forgot all about the crowd. He read like he wrote, as though Grandma was right there and he was telling her about his adventure. He was dimly aware that the audience oohed and aahed and laughed at all the right places. When he was finished the audience cheered. Sam sat down. *Not too shabby,* he thought.

Another girl read, but Sam didn't even hear her. He was too busy daydreaming about the new X-Treme Trail Smasher he was sure would be his.

Billy read last. His essay was about a trip across the bay to Fossil Point with his dad. They collected huge rocks full of fish and clam fossils to decorate the chimney of the fireplace they were building in their new house. Their old house had burned in the forest fire and as Billy read, Sam could see people in the audience wiping away tears.

Billy finished with an inspiring message about not letting a tragedy—like losing your house in a fire—get you down. Instead you should look ahead and rebuild your life. Not only did the audience applaud, several people jumped to their feet and cheered.

Sam's heart sank. He was foolish to think he ever had a chance to win the grand prize!

The principal said a few more words about how proud he was of the finalists. *Okay, okay,* thought Sam, *just get to the winners!*

But no, the principal went on and on. He

thanked the judges. He thanked the teachers. He thanked the parents. Sam thought he would explode he was so impatient!

Finally it was time. One of the judges handed the principal a card. "Third place goes to Mary Rutledge," he announced. Mary accepted her twenty-five dollar prize with a grin.

"And second place . . ." began the principal. Sam closed his eyes, expecting to hear his name. He thought to himself that the fifty-dollar prize for second place was better than nothing. ". . . goes to Billy Sutton," the principal finished.

Sam's eyes flew open. *Billy? Does that mean I didn't win anything?* he wondered. His head was spinning. *Maybe my essay was no good after all . . .*

But then Sam heard the words, "And the two-hundred-dollar first prize goes to . . . Sam Peterson!" He had won!

Sam was in a daze as he walked to the podium and shook the principal's hand. "Congratulations, Sam," said the principal and he handed Sam an envelope.

The envelope! Inside it was two hundred dollars! With that money, plus his savings, Sam could finally buy the X-Treme Trail Smasher bike! The audience applauded, and Sam looked out, grinned a giant grin, and bowed deeply. The audience laughed and cheered.

In the crush of people leaving the gym, Sam found Mom and Dad. They hugged him and congratulated him.

"We made a big blueberry pie to celebrate," said Dad.

"And we invited Billy and his folks over for dessert," added Mom. "Let's go."

Sam didn't need to be convinced. He was starving. The Suttons were already at the house when Sam and his parents arrived.

After lots of handshaking and backslapping, they sat down to the best blueberry pie Sam had ever tasted: tangy blueberries, a flaky cinnamon-sugar crust, and vanilla ice cream melting alongside.

Sam and Billy talked about what they would buy at the bike shop in Homer. Billy wanted a fancy bike pump so he could fill his tires without going to the gas station. Sam wondered what color X-Treme Trail Smasher he would get.

Just then, Neptune wandered in with something in her mouth. It was black and fuzzy and covered with drool.

"Eeewww," cried Billy. "What's that?"

Sam looked closely, then laughed. "It's my old bear. Last night I pulled it out of the closet for good luck. Now I guess it belongs to you, Neptune. I seem to have all the good luck I need!"

Neptune wagged her tail and trotted

over to the woodstove. She lay down with the soggy old bear between her paws. Sam and Billy helped themselves to another piece of pie and joined Neptune in front of the fire. They spent the rest of the evening planning all the places they would explore on their X-Treme Trail Smashers—places far away from any blueberry bears!